Carol

DONALD

AND

THE SECRET SCROLL

Illustrations by
Alec Wills

550669283 1

Published by Lulu, 2013

Cover design by Alec Wills

Lulu Books

DONALD AND THE SECRET SCROLL

He woke suddenly – something had disturbed him. There was a tinkering noise outside the caravan. His thoughts went first of all to the little black and white duck. The sound continued, like a tap tapping of a beak on the caravan door. He turned over and tried to get back to sleep, but then, he heard the sound of something being dropped. He sat up; that didn't sound like Tufty. He would have to take a look.

This second book in the 'Donald' series will continue to delight children of around eight years. All their favourite characters are back at 'Signor Pepperino's Amazing Circus,' finding themselves with yet another mystery to solve.

Contents

Victor Vulcan

Victor Vulcan, the legendary trapeze artist, famous for his dare-devil stunts was coming to 'Signor Pepperino's Amazing Circus.' He had delighted audiences all around the world and was at this moment on his way to Broadland. He was to be blasted out of a canon, at break neck speed, to the high wire of the Big Top. Signor Pepperino's circus was buzzing with excitement.

Donald, the circus boy, was as thrilled as everyone else and was busy putting up posters advertising this incredible new act. He couldn't wait to tell his friend, Jen.

Leaving his cat, Henry, behind in the caravan, he ran along the marshy track, over the broken stile, to the houseboat at the side of the river. This was where Jen spent the summer, with her Uncle Bob, the ferryman, and Chikitta, his monkey.

Donald had been part of 'Signor Pepperino's Amazing Circus' for over a year now and with each passing season, the circus' reputation had grown and grown. They had now returned to Broadland for the summer and he was particularly looking forward to seeing the ferryman's monkey whom he had rescued last year from the old windmill.

As Donald arrived at the muddy creek, the memories of last summer and the delights of Broadland all came flooding back. This was going to be a very special summer indeed and he didn't want to waste a moment of it.

A blast of banana suddenly shot through the air and onto Donald's forehead.

"Chikitta," shouted Donald happily.

The monkey jumped onto his shoulder and patted his head affectionately with her hands.

Immediately, there erupted another burst of excitement, which bounded towards Donald with even more energy than the super-sonic banana. It was Jen. Her dark curls bounced around her shoulders and her bright eyes shone warmly at him.

"Uncle Bob said that you were arriving today. I don't know who is most pleased to see you; me or Cheeky Keeta."

Chikitta sprang away from Donald, and into the trees, flicking furry catkins at the children before turning to wave a cheeky pink bottom in their faces.

"Some things never change," laughed Donald. "So when did you arrive? What about Charlie and Josh? Are they coming to spend the summer here too?"

"Hey, not so many questions. I came yesterday, and Charlie and Josh are joining us next week."

Donald was pleased. Charlie and Josh had helped rescue Chikitta last year and with them all together again it would be just like old times.

"So how are things at 'Signor Pepperino's Amazing Circus'?" asked Jen.

"You can come and see if you like. Oh, and you've not met Twitch yet. He's my new rabbit. I think Signor Pepperino gave him to me as a kind of replacement for Chikitta. He's a bit nervous, but cute once you get to know him, and he gets on really well with Henry."

"That's a relief."

They both remembered how wary Henry had been of Chikitta, which was not surprising as there was nothing that she liked to do more than to annoy the poor cat.

"Come on, let's go and find them." Donald held out his hand for the monkey and the three of them ran back over the broken stile, along the marshy track, to the circus which had become Donald's home.

"I hope Henry's ready for this," said Donald, grimly. He pushed open his caravan door and put his finger to his lips. There on the window sill lay Henry, in his usual position, and curled up, between his two sandy coloured front paws was the little white rabbit.

It was a whole year since the little brown monkey had been in Donald's caravan and she was very excited to be back. She leapt through the door, grabbed a squishy orange and hurled it at the window, just above Henry. Unfortunately, the window was open and Signor Pepperino just happened to be ambling by. It smacked him right in the face. Before Signor Pepperino had a chance to recover from the shock of an orange, splattered all over his nose, two other missiles came hurtling towards him; one was a cat and the other was a rabbit.

"Ah, Bambino, what is this? It is raining cats and rabbits and oranges all at once!"

Chikitta suddenly appeared on the window sill and she jumped and chattered at Signor Pepperino, who groaned. "I might have guessed." He wiped the last traces of orange from his face.

"Hello Signor Pepperino," said Jen, trying not to laugh.

"Ah Jen, how delightful to see you. How is your uncle?"

"Very well thank you and I think that he is hoping to see you at the houseboat later on."

"Excellent. We will go down this evening." Signor Pepperino turned to Donald. "Now Bambino, have you told Jen our exciting news?"

"No, but I was about to." Donald proudly pointed to a poster which was lying on his bed.

"Victor Vulcan," exclaimed Jen. "I've heard of him."

"Everyone's heard of him," said Donald, enthusiastically. "He's arriving today and just think; he's joining our circus for the summer."

"Well, I'm not surprised," said Jen. "Signor Pepperino's circus has got to be the best circus anywhere."

"I wonder if I'll ever be on the stage with the famous Victor Vulcan."

"Ah, there's no reason why not Bambino. Just wait and see." Signor Pepperino then left as he needed to make sure that his circus was ready for their very distinguished visitor.

"Come on," said Donald. "I'll take you to see the caravan that's being prepared for him. It's right at the other side of the field."

The caravan that they arrived at was large and decorative and it stood slightly apart from the others. People were fussing around, constantly hustling and bustling back and forth, making sure that it was swept and tidied, polished and cleaned. It was now gleaming like a ringmaster's new top hat.

"Gosh, it's even bigger and brighter than Signor Pepperino's caravan," said Jen. "When's he arriving?"

"Any time now I guess," said Donald, feeling a bit bemused by all the activity.

Suddenly, the caravan cleared of people and everything went strangely quiet. Donald turned round to see Signor Pepperino and a much taller person walking towards them.

"Is that him?" whispered Jen, giving Donald a nudge. "He looks very grand."

Donald's mouth dropped open and he stepped aside.

Signor Pepperino and Victor Vulcan walked up the two steps into the caravan. The door closed and all the curious onlookers slowly melted away.

Chikitta and the Tie

The warm crimson glow of evening time drew Donald back along the marshy track, over the broken stile, to the houseboat at the side of the river. He was looking forward to supper with the ferryman and he was already breathing the smell of sizzling sausages, which mingled with the clean, fresh air of Broadland.

Jen had returned to the houseboat a few hours earlier and Donald had grown tired of waiting for Signor Pepperino. No doubt he still had things to sort out with their very special guest.

Henry was running at Donald's feet and was the first to reach the houseboat. He jumped onto the roof, where he had a 'cat's eye' view. If there were any troublesome monkeys around, he would be the first to see.

Donald was immediately handed a sausage by Jen and he helped himself to a roll, tomato ketchup and plenty of crispy onions.

"Good to see you laddie," said the ferryman as he walked out onto the deck. "Is Signor Pepperino not joining us? Jen and I have been looking forward to his special elderberry juice and chocolate muffins."

"I'm sure he won't be long," replied Donald. "He was still with Victor Vulcan, so I decided to come on my own – and with Henry of course."

"Victor Vulcan is the famous trapeze artist," explained Jen. "He's joining Signor Pepperino's circus for the summer."

Chikitta suddenly started to jump around excitedly and then she sprang up onto the roof of the boat. Henry immediately disappeared.

Donald looked around to see what had disturbed her and to his surprise, he saw two men walking towards the riverbank. They wore dark suits and flashy ties which, to Donald, seemed strange amongst the brambles and bushes of the muddy creek.

The men ignored Donald and Jen, and turned their attention to Bob, the ferryman.

"A lovely evening," remarked the man with the bright, purple coloured, zig zaggy tie.

"Hmm, it was nice and peaceful," said the ferryman gruffly.

The other man, with the green spotty tie forced a laugh, and walked up to the houseboat. "It's your lucky day," he said, smiling. "We've come to make you a very desirable offer."

"I'll be the judge of that," grunted the ferryman. "What's all this about?"

"We've taken ownership of all the moorings up this stretch of the creek and we understand that this little patch belongs to you."

The zig zaggy tie hung over the side of the boat and flapped as the man enthusiastically waved a piece of paper in the air.

"We are prepared to offer you a new mooring, well away from here, and a generous sum of money in return for this muddy puddle."

His podgy finger pointed at the page. "You just have to sign right here."

Chikitta was still chattering agitatedly. Donald climbed out onto the roof and patted her gently in an effort to calm her down. He wasn't sure what this was all about, but he felt that these two visitors were not exactly welcome. Donald remembered how gruff the old ferryman had been when he had first met him last summer … and he seemed much crosser today.

"Now, listen here," said the ferryman, glaring at the two men. "This muddy puddle happens to be my home and no-one is taking it from me. Chikitta and I manage well enough without your money, so if you'll excuse me, I'd like to get back to my supper."

The two once smiling faces exchanged glances.

"I'm afraid you don't understand," said the man with the spotty tie. "Things are about to change around here; time is moving on. We are only concerned with what is best for you."

"Go on, be off with you. I'm going no-where."

The man with the spotty tie stood up stiffly. "Well I'm sorry that you take that attitude. It's always best to move with the times. I'm afraid we'll be back."

The bright, shiny zigzags were still dangling over the boat and had caught a monkey's beady eye. Chikitta suddenly leapt from the roof of the houseboat towards the zig zaggy material. She caught it in her hand and swung herself around the man's neck and over his head; then she let go and catapulted herself to the top of an over-hanging tree.

An explosion of spluttering and choking followed as the man grabbed at the neck of his shirt. He glared at the old man and then at Chikitta, who was swaying around in the tree, waving a cheeky pink bottom in his face.

He shook his fist at her before turning to the ferryman. "I'm reporting that monkey. You'll be without that 'fleabag' and without a home by the end of the month."

Uncle Bob, the two children, a monkey and a cat, watched the two visitors in their dark suits and their flashy ties disappear up the marshy track, over the broken stile, and towards 'Signor Pepperino's Amazing Circus.' They didn't seem to have even noticed the plump, smiley ringmaster, with a twirling moustache who passed them.

Chikitta, hanging by her tail, threw catkins down at Signor Pepperino as he reached the boat.

Signor Pepperino stepped onto the houseboat with a bottle of elderberry juice and a feast of chocolate muffins and together, they settled down for supper.

They talked about Victor Vulcan until late into the evening. Donald noticed that the ferryman didn't mention the two visitors, so he thought that he had better keep the incident to himself.

Donald Meets Victor Vulcan

Donald hadn't slept much that night and he didn't feel like breakfast this morning. He put it down to nerves.

Whilst walking back to the circus with Signor Pepperino the previous evening, he'd had some exciting news. Victor Vulcan wanted to meet with him this morning … to try out some ideas for his new act.

Donald's initial enthusiasm was beginning to wear off. The thought of performing with the famous Victor Vulcan terrified him. Slowly, with his unicycle under his arm, and with Henry at his heels, he made his way to the brightly coloured caravan across the field. He knew that he was early, but he knocked on the door.

He was met by a tall man with thick brown hair.

"You must be Donald," he said, smiling. "Signor Pepperino has spoken a great deal about you."

He glanced at the unicycle that Donald was carrying. "You won't need that. Keep it for your clown routines. I require a trapeze artist."

Donald couldn't believe his ears. He felt flattered but wondered why Victor Vulcan hadn't asked one of Signor Pepperino's real trapeze artists. He pushed the thought from his mind. Victor Vulcan had chosen him and that was what mattered. He followed the great man inside the caravan. All around, there were posters and articles of 'The Vulcan's' bold feats, hanging from the walls.

Donald sat down. He watched as 'The Vulcan' moved around the caravan. He seemed like a giant, with strong, muscular arms. Donald suddenly felt very small.

A chocolate milkshake was handed to him. Donald took it gratefully; having missed breakfast, he was now feeling hungry.

'The Vulcan' sat down.

"You see, it's like this. People are used to seeing me flying out of canons and looping the loop on the high wire. I want something different, but equally daring; equally spectacular. Something that the audiences of Broadland will never forget."

"But what has all this got to do with me?"

The tall, muscular man leaned closer. "What if a little person were to shoot out of the canon? A child could go further, higher – imagine it … and it could be you."

Donald was dumbfounded. This was way beyond anything that he had done before … and it sounded dangerous. He couldn't agree; he couldn't disagree. The strong, powerful face was still smiling at him.

"What does Signor Pepperino think?" asked Donald, thinking that if the great ringmaster agreed, then it must be alright.

Victor Vulcan leaned across, even closer and put his finger to his lips.

"It's a surprise," he said. "Signor Pepperino speaks very highly of you and is happy for me to include you in my act. He doesn't know that I intend to put you in the starring role. Signor Pepperino will be amazed; audiences will be swept off their feet. What do you say?"

Donald felt proud. Even Signor Pepperino hadn't spoken to him like this before. He nodded enthusiastically, but was interrupted by Henry, pulling at his trousers.

"Stop it Henry," said Donald, trying to shoo the cat away by flicking his ankle. "What's wrong with you?"

Victor Vulcan bent down to help. He tried to pick the cat up, but Henry still clung onto the bottom of Donald's trousers. He tried clapping his hands in front of the cat's face in an attempt to distract him.

Henry suddenly let go and turned to face the big man. His fur stood up in pointed prickles and his tail rose and waved threateningly from side to side.

"I'm sorry," stammered Donald. "I don't know what's got into him. Henry doesn't usually behave like this."

"Come on Henry," said Donald quickly. "I think we'd better go."

As Donald reached the caravan door, he turned back to the famous trapeze artist. "When do we start?" he asked nervously.

"How about this afternoon? I'll meet you at 2 o'clock in the Big Top."

By the time Donald had reached his caravan, he had forgotten all about Henry's strange behaviour. He couldn't believe that he had been chosen to perform with the famous Victor Vulcan. Whatever would Jen think?

Frankie and Tom, the two other circus clowns were waiting for Donald when he arrived back at his caravan.

"We need to sort out some rehearsal times," said Tom. "There's only a week until our first show."

Donald nodded absently. "I'm busy today; maybe tomorrow."

***

Donald arrived at the Big Top in plenty of time. He'd left Henry behind with Twitch; he didn't want to risk another scene. He couldn't understand what could have made him behave so badly.

The curtain flapped open and Donald looked round eagerly; he couldn't wait to start. To his dismay, it was not Victor Vulcan.

"Great; you've changed your mind," said Frankie. "We were going to have a short practice without you, but now you're here…"

Tom leapt over onto the trampoline.

The curtain flapped open once again and a much taller figure walked inside.

"Sorry guys; Big Top's booked for this afternoon." He nodded at Donald. "You'll have to find another time for clowning around. We've some tricky stunts to work on."

Donald looked at the ground and turned red. He could feel the other two clowns staring at him. They left without any fuss.

Donald breathed a sigh of relief and waited to be told what to do.

"We need to get you confident on the high wire," said 'The Vulcan.' "We can't even attempt the canon until I can trust you up there."

The next few hours were spent balancing and swinging; catching ropes and falling into safety nets. By the end of the practice, Donald was exhausted. Victor Vulcan, on the other hand, had kept his feet firmly on the ground, and he was not exhausted at all.

Broadshaven Bridge

Donald had never been to the bridge at Broadshaven before, which made the planned trip all the more exciting. He and Henry were down at the water's edge bright and early.

Jen had the lunch packed and life jackets at the ready; Uncle Bob was there to release the mooring rope from the tree.

"Now remember," he said. "You're going on a falling tide; make sure that you come back with the in-coming tide – it turns at 4 o'clock this afternoon."

Jen nodded. She'd been brought up with the knowledge that you work *with* the tides on Broadland's rivers.

They pushed away from the bank and Jen began to row up the muddy creek towards the larger broad that they had been on the previous summer.

"Hey, where's Chikitta?"

"She's in disgrace. Uncle Bob is still cross with her for swinging round that man's neck. She's 'boat bound' for one whole day."

"Poor Chikitta. Oh well, at least Henry will be pleased – not that he deserves to be. He's been misbehaving too."

"What do you mean?"

"He was spitting and growling yesterday in Victor Vulcan's caravan."

"Gosh, that's not like Henry. Whatever was he doing in there?"

"It's very exciting. I'm taking part in his new act. I'm going to fly out of the canon … but don't tell anyone; even Signor Pepperino doesn't know yet."

"That's amazing, but why can't you tell Signor Pepperino?"

"It's supposed to be a surprise."

"Oh, I see. Hey look, we've reached the broad already; it'll be easy from now on, just a case of drifting with the tide."

The sun was warm and the gentle north easterly breeze was blowing them in the direction that they wanted to go; progress was swift and they reached the bridge well before lunch time.

Jen steered the boat to the bank and tied it to a mooring post; then she passed the lunch and the cat out to Donald, who was already on the bank.

They made their way across the grassy slope, to the bottom of the old stone bridge. The soft, rustic colours were patched with tufts of greeny moss, which grew there in the damp and the shade.

Henry decided to go instead to the top of the bridge, where he stretched out in the midday sunshine.

Underneath the arch, there was a ledge of rock, running along one side. Donald and

Jen found it a good place to sit. Their feet touched the water and green tassels of willow branches screened them on either side from the many picnickers who dotted the grassy banks. This felt to Donald like a secret hide-out and the perfect place to eat their lunch.

Jen handed Donald a cheese and onion roll and some of Signor Pepperino's elderberry juice. Suddenly, the cup seemed to jerk out of her hand and the thick, red drink spilt into the river. The water instantly turned red.

"Sorry," she said. "One of these stones wobbled." She gave them a push to find which one had moved. To her surprise, the loose stone jiggled a bit more and then came away in her hand. A little dark compartment was left in its place.

"What do you suppose is in there?" she asked.

"Slugs and snails..." said Donald, prodding the hole with a stick, "... spiders and beetles." He felt something in the corner and heard a crunch as he jabbed it. He put his hand inside and pulled out a brown envelope.

"What is it?"

Donald lay the mystery package down on the ledge.

"It's only folded down," said Jen. "Let's have a quick look inside and then we can put it straight back."

Donald didn't need persuading. He carefully unwrapped the folds of the envelope and took out a piece of paper.

"It's a map," said Jen, peering over, "of the broads. Look, here are the mooring posts at the muddy creek – this one is Uncle Bob's."

Donald looked more closely. "Hey, this wiggly line must be the marshy track." He pointed at a patch of green at the other end of the wiggly line. "And this must be the site of the circus."

"Why is it all highlighted in red?" asked Jen.

"I don't know." Donald looked round uneasily. He felt that he was somehow intruding. "I think we'd better put it back now."

He returned the map to the envelope and carefully folded the top down as it was before. Then he returned it to the hole and fitted the stone back into place.

"Let's go and sit on the grass," he said, "and see if anyone comes to collect it. It could have been left for someone to pick up in secret."

They made their way back up the bank.

A black and white crested duck drifted underneath the arch with the current; fish darted amongst the reeds and young children splashed around with their sticks and their nets in the grey and white dappled water as it trickled over its bed of stones.

No-one seemed to be interested in their rocky ledge, or in the stone that wobbled just above it.

After a while, Jen grew restless and wandered up to where Henry was still lying, on the wall of the bridge. From here, she could see the hustle and bustle of the busy little tourist town of Broadshaven, as people sat and drank outside cafes; browsed in and out of shops and queued for ice-creams. Suddenly, she turned back to Donald and beckoned him over. "Come here, quickly! Look, it's a good job Chikitta's not here."

She was pointing to the other side of the road, where two men were leaving the Wherrie Inn. They were casually dressed today, but Donald recognised them straight away.

"They're the men who came to see Uncle Bob," she said. "I wonder if they've come to collect the envelope."

The two children held their breath as the men walked across the road, towards the grassy bank. Once they had crossed over however, they got into a silver car, which took them away from Broadshaven and away from the two watching children.

"Well, that's that," said Donald.

"And it's 4 o'clock," said Jen. "We need to go now if we're going to catch the tide back up to the creek."

Donald took the oars on the way back. "I felt sure that they would collect the package," he said disappointedly. "They were interested in the muddy creek after all."

"Maybe they were the ones who left it there – for someone else to collect."

"I guess we'll never know."

Henry was more interested in the black and white crested duck, which had been following them up the river. His fur bristled and his tail waved from side to side, while the duck made little *currah currah* noises back at him.

***

It was Chikitta who was the first to meet the children back at the muddy creek. She jumped straight into Donald's lap before he even had time to get out of the boat.

"It looks like she's been forgiven," said Jen.

Henry looked warily from the duck, to Chikitta and decided to make a quick exit. He jumped onto the river bank and away from his tormentors.

Donald and Henry were soon making their way back over the broken stile, along the marshy track, to the circus. As they reached the caravan, Donald saw Frankie and Tom walking towards him and his heart sank. He'd forgotten that he was supposed to have met them this afternoon for a practice at the Big Top.

"I presume you're still too busy for us," said Frankie.

Donald looked down at his feet. "I'm sorry," he mumbled. "I did mean to come."

"Perhaps you might manage to remember tomorrow morning," said Tom sarcastically. Then they left.

Donald knew that he should have got back earlier. He would definitely make it up to them in the morning. He would make sure that he was the first one to arrive at the Big Top. He would prove to them that he still wanted to be one of the clowns of 'Signor Pepperino's Amazing Circus.'

The Big Top

There was no chance of Donald sleeping in. Chikitta was tapping at his window bright and early. He stirred himself and went to open it. The little brown monkey jumped inside just as Henry jumped out. She grabbed some oranges and began to juggle.

Donald remembered that the last time Chikitta had come to find him, it was because she needed help; the ferryman had fallen and hurt himself. Today however, she seemed quite relaxed. Oranges were flying fast and furious from hand to tail until Donald finally stepped in.

"Come on," he said firmly, gathering the fruit back into the bowl. "You may as well come to the Big Top with me. We can have a short practise before breakfast and before Frankie and Tom arrive."

With Chikitta holding one hand, and his unicycle in the other, they made their way to the Big Top.

The circus felt very different at this time of day. Donald could feel the grass, still wet with dew through his sandals and everywhere was quiet. Even Signor Pepperino's caravan showed no signs of activity. Donald was pleased. He wanted time to practise alone.

He pulled back the flap of the Big Top and went inside. Blinds were pulled down low over the clear canvas windows and the stage was in shadow.

A rustling noise broke the silence and Chikitta jumped into his arms. There was a tall figure amongst the ropes and wires; busy in the half light.

Donald had the strange feeling that he shouldn't be here … he didn't want to be seen. He wondered who else was up at this time – in the Big Top, when no-one else was about. The image hung tall and heavy in the gloom. He was sure that it couldn't be Signor Pepperino and neither did it look like Frankie or Tom. The two of them remained huddled together. Donald could feel the furry body in his arms trembling slightly and it made him feel uneasy. He was determined to stay hidden.

He breathed a sigh of relief when the dark figure suddenly got up, walked over to the entrance, and disappeared. Donald and Chikitta were left alone.

Chikitta leapt out of Donald's arms and swung her way up the ropes to the high wire. From here, she hung from her tail and clapped her hands, wondering why there was no-one else to applaud her acrobatics.

"Very clever," said Donald. "You've given me a good idea for our new act."

They spent much time working on a familiar stunt, but with Chikitta playing the starring role. Donald circled the trampoline on his unicycle, with Chikitta on his shoulders. Once he started up the ramp, Chikitta sprang into the air. She worked her way up a rope, until she was dangling by her tail from the high wire. She waited for Donald to pedal across the trampoline, and then dropped down and landed on the floor next to him. Her timing was perfect.

"Well done," said Donald, giving her a hug. "You just need to make sure that you don't collide with Frankie or Tom."

He was sure that she would manage this. Monkey acrobatics came naturally to her after all.

Donald was circling around the arena for a final turn up the ramp when a familiar figure walked through the flap and called out to him.

"Ah Bambino, here you are; I have been looking for you. Victor Vulcan is joining us for breakfast."

"Donald jumped off his unicycle and ran over to the great ringmaster. "I wanted to practise early," he explained, "before I meet with Frankie and Tom." He looked at his watch. "Gosh, they'll be here in an hour."

"Ah well, come quickly Bambino. You can't perform properly if you don't eat."

Soon the three of them were making their way to Signor Pepperino's caravan. The window was open and Donald could smell the bacon well before they arrived. He suddenly felt very ready for breakfast. "What about Chikitta?" he asked.

"Hmm, I expect I can rustle up something for a monkey."

Victor Vulcan smiled at Donald as he walked in. He also tapped his nose, discreetly. Donald knew that this was a sign that he was not to mention the new act to Signor Peperino. He hadn't forgotten. He wondered what the ringmaster would think when he came soaring out of the canon.

Soon they were all tucking into crispy

bacon and scrambled eggs. Chikitta was unusually quiet. No-one was aware of the bowl of trifle at the front of the fridge that had taken her fancy. She had wasted no time in finding out how good it tasted. Raspberries, custard and cream were spread all over her face.

"Don't forget Chikitta?" said Donald suddenly. "She'll be hungry too."

Knowing that she was being talked about, Chikitta hopped under the table. Fluffs of yellow, white and red flew after her.

"Oh Chikitta," said Donald sternly. "That wasn't for you."

"Ah, that pesky monkey," said Signor Pepperino, getting up and shooing her out from under the table. He began to clear up the bits of trifle that had splattered around the caravan. Donald took a tissue and wiped her red and white blotchy face. Victor Vulcan looked on but said nothing.

Donald decided that it was time to go. He knew that Frankie and Tom would be expecting him, so, taking Chikitta's hand, the two of them made their way across the circus to the Big Top.

The Hiding Place

Donald and Chikitta walked back to the caravan. The practice with Frankie and Tom had gone well; Chikitta had more than made up for stealing the trifle. Her swings were effortless and her timing perfect. Donald knew that Signor Pepperino would be proud of her. He was also relieved to find that Frankie and Tom no longer seemed annoyed. They were all back together, doing what they were good at, and Signor Pepperino had an act that he could be proud of.

Chikitta suddenly leapt away from Donald as Jen came running towards them.

"Thank goodness; she's with you." Jen bent down to pick the little brown monkey up in her arms.

"What's the matter?"

"Those two men are back. Uncle Bob's had a terrible row with them – he won't sign their piece of paper and now they want Chikitta. Apparently they've reported her to the police – said she's a danger to the public."

"That's ridiculous."

"I know, but the police might not see it like that. Uncle Bob will be so upset if they take her away."

"Don't worry. No-one is taking Chikitta anywhere; she can stay here."

"That won't help; they're on their way … to find her."

"Then we'll keep her hidden," said Donald firmly.

"But where?"

By now, the three of them had reached the caravan. Donald looked round despairingly as Chiktta hopped through the window and started juggling plates. However was he supposed to hide such a lively monkey?

Suddenly, she jumped back out with a plate in her hand. She threw it 'Frisbee style' through the open door of the rabbit hutch, which stood on a bench just outside. Twitch, who had been quietly nibbling on some hay, froze for a second, and then bolted, disappearing underneath the caravan.

Jen looked at Donald. He knew exactly what she was thinking. "I know it won't be easy."

"It'll be impossible. She never keeps still for a moment."

Just then, two jazzy ties; one zig zaggy and the other spotty, were flapping their way towards them. In between the two smug looking men, was Signor Pepperino. He looked very serious.

Donald looked down at Chikitta just as she jumped into the hutch after her plate. He quickly slammed the door shut and stood there, with his back to it.

"Ah Bambino, I have some very bad news. That monkey; she's been misbehaving, inexcusably. Not only does she steal trifles, but apparently, she tried to strangle this poor gentleman."

The man with the zig zaggy tie wore a forlorn kind of smile, while his eyes darted around eagerly, no doubt looking for any signs of the missing monkey.

"I ... I'm sure she didn't mean to," stammered Donald.

Signor Pepperino shook his head. "I'm afraid Bambino, this time she's gone too far. The police have requested that in the interest of the general public, she should be handed in; so that she can be kept properly under control."

Donald kept his back to the hutch as he wondered what he should do. Then, his eyes met Signor Pepperino's and Donald knew that the great ringmaster was on his side.

"Um, she doesn't seem to be here," he said, keeping his eyes fixed on Signor Pepperino. "You know what she's like; here today, making mischief somewhere else tomorrow."

Signor Pepperino's eyes twinkled back at Donald. There was an unspoken understanding between them. They both knew that Signor Pepperino had said these words himself last summer, when Chikitta had been kidnapped by the ticket man from the old windmill. Donald had rescued her once. He wasn't going to lose her again.

"Well Bambino, if I see any sign of her, it will be my duty to turn her over to the police." He raised his eyebrows and gave a little nod.

Donald knew that this was the ringmaster's way of warning him to keep Chikitta hidden. Neither Signor Pepperino nor the ferryman would want her to be handed over to the police.

"Ah and Bambino … a message from Victor Vulcan. He says that he will meet you tomorrow morning, in the Big Top."

Then Signor Pepperino shook hands with the two men and walked away. He had a busy day ahead of him.

Donald and Jen stood there uneasily.

"You've not seen the last of us," said the man with the zig zaggy tie. "We'll find her … and when we do, we'll lock her up and throw away the key."

At last they left and Donald breathed a sigh of relief. Once they were out of sight, he opened up the hutch and took Chikitta in his arms.

"Good old Cheeky Keeta," said Jen. "I would never have believed that she could keep so quiet."

"You understand don't you," said Donald, looking into the little monkey's eyes. "They mustn't find you."

Chikitta whimpered and then jumped back into the hutch.

"Seems as good a hiding place as any," said Donald grinning. "No-one would think of looking for a monkey in a rabbit hutch. I'm not sure what Twitch will think of it though."

He bent down to look underneath the caravan, but the little white rabbit had gone. They soon found him curled up on the window sill, next to Henry.

"Perhaps he could manage without a hutch for a while," suggested Jen.

Tufty

Keeping Chikitta hidden was not nearly as difficult as Donald had thought it would be. She seemed to actually like the rabbit hutch, particularly when Henry came to lie down on top. Her favourite pastime had become pushing pieces of straw through the wire at Henry's drooping tail. She had learnt that if she poked ever so gently, the tail would flicker a bit and Henry would stir just enough to keep things interesting. The game could keep the monkey amused for half an hour at least.

Twitch was also enjoying himself and managing very well without a hutch. He seemed to approve of his new home in the caravan. Donald had provided him with a big box, filled with straw and hay, and he could go inside whenever he wished.

Donald enjoyed having Twitch around. He seemed to have become much less nervous and had even taken to following him around the circus – almost as much as Henry.

Today, the rabbit was sitting on the windowsill, munching on some lettuce that Signor Pepperino had brought him as a special treat. He was watching Henry who was sprawled across the top of the hutch, and in particular, the creamy tipped tail as it flipped back and forth.

Donald was wondering where he should take Chikitta today. Much as she liked the rabbit hutch, he couldn't expect her to stay in there all day. Suddenly, he was distracted by a tapping noise at the side of the caravan. He went outside to have a look. There were several pieces of straw being poked through the rabbit hutch, but otherwise, there seemed to be nothing out of place. He went back inside.

The next time the tapping started, it was accompanied by a soft whistling. He went back outside to find a small black and white duck, with a silky tuft on the top of its head.

The duck padded up to Donald and then spread his wings and flapped his way through the caravan door. The noise startled

Henry and he quickly disappeared onto the roof of the caravan. Chikitta sat at the back of the hutch, sulking and threading the strands of straw around her own tail.

Donald, feeling slightly bemused, followed the duck inside. Even Twitch had stopped nibbling to take a look.

"A caravan's no place for a duck," he said firmly. "I think I'd better take you down to the muddy creek. Come on; we may as well go now, while it's still quiet."

The black and white duck obediently followed Donald out of the caravan and over to the rabbit hutch, where Chikitta was still sulking.

"Come on Chikitta," whispered Donald. "We're going to take Tufty to the muddy creek."

The crest of feathers on top of the duck's head was fluttering in the breeze and the name had slipped out quite naturally.

Chikitta, having had her game interrupted didn't intend to take Tufty anywhere. She turned away.

"Oh come on Chikitta; don't be like that. You'll be able to see Jen."

The monkey sat still for a moment, and then pushed open the door and took Donald's hand. Twitch returned to his lettuce and Henry barely opened a sleepy eye as they left.

Donald, Chikitta and a black and white duck padded their way along the marshy track, over the broken stile, to the houseboat at the side of the river. Jen came out onto the deck to meet them. It didn't take her long to notice the duck.

"Meet Tufty," said Donald. "He seems to have lost his way; ended up in my caravan."

"He looks like the duck that was following us up the river when we came back from the bridge. I recognise those grey speckly bits."

"Well, I wonder what he's doing here."

Chikitta was already up in the trees, throwing furry catkins as close to the speckly bits as she could.

"How's Cheeky Keeta been?" asked Jen. "Any trouble?"

"She's been very good, but doesn't seem too keen on Tufty."

The catkins were by now coming by the handful and the duck slipped into the water.

"So what are we going to do with her today?" asked Jen. "We can't keep her here."

"Let's follow Tufty, in the rowing boat. She did come and find me after all."

Jen disappeared back into the cabin and returned with Uncle Bob and two life jackets.

"Hello laddie. I guessed you'd be down sooner or later. Any signs of dangerous monkeys?" he winked as yet another fistful of catkins came hurtling towards them.

"None at all," said Donald, grinning.

"You can take the boat," the old man continued, "providing you wait for me to do you both some lunch."

By the time the rowing boat was ready, the ferryman was at the water's edge with a large bag.

"That should keep you going," he said, handing it over. "And don't forget the tides; one hour later today."

The children waved as they pushed out from the bank. They rowed down the river after a little black and white duck with a grey speckled crest, which fluttered in the breeze.

"She seems to be heading back to the bridge," said Jen.

The wind was in their face today and they didn't make quite such good progress, but the duck waited for them and kept pace with the rowing boat all the way. It wasn't until they reached the bridge at Broadshaven that he bobbed over to the reeds at the side of the river. Donald and Jen drifted over to the mooring post.

"Shall we have our picnic at the bridge?" asked Donald.

"We may as well. We can keep Cheeky Keeta hidden better down there and anyway, that's where Tufty has gone."

Jen handed Donald the bag of food and, with Chikitta between them, they ran across the grassy slope, to the narrow ledge under the bridge. Chikitta balanced herself on a willow branch, with her tail swinging just above the water.

The lunch that the ferryman had packed was a real feast. There were sausage rolls, slabs of cheese and slices of ham; there were crisps and cakes, as well as a container crammed full of cherries – not to mention two bottles of elderberry juice.

It was quiet underneath the bridge. The children were too busy eating to talk and

Chikitta was busy foraging around amongst the trees and bushes.

"I couldn't eat another thing," said Donald eventually, "and there's still a packet of cakes left."

"We can always have them for tea. We don't have to leave till later today – tide turns at five."

Neither of them spoke for a while, but each knew what the other was thinking. Jen pushed on the wobbly stone. Donald glanced between the weeping willow branches.

"Go on then," he said. "Let's see if the envelope's still there."

Jen carefully jiggled the stone until it became loose in her hand. She began to wriggle her fingers around in the hole and then snatched them away. "I can't help thinking about those spiders and snails."

Donald shuffled along the ledge. "I'll do it." He put his hand into the hole and felt into all the corners. He shook his head. "It's gone."

"Are you sure? Try with this." Jen handed him a stick.

Donald scraped the stick around until they were both convinced that the envelope was no longer there.

Jen carefully replaced the stone into the wall of the bridge. The duck was still swimming round, making little *currah, currah* noises at them.

The afternoon passed pleasantly. The wind had dropped and it felt to the children, like the first really hot day of the summer. The river was busy with canoes and sailing boats, while swans glided past, in the shade of the rushes.

The tide was slack and after having enjoyed a swim, they decided that it was time for an ice cream. As they walked up the grassy slope, they could already feel their soaking wet clothes drying in the hot sun.

"I hope Cheeky Keeta keeps herself hidden."

"She'll be fine in the trees. She blends in well with the branches."

***

It was while the children were standing in the queue, waiting for their ice creams, that two,

smartly dressed men walked across the road,
down the grassy slope, towards the bridge.
One of them had something in his hand.

Two beady eyes were watching them
from the branches of the willow tree.

Shadows at Midnight

The two men sat down on a bench. It was just a short distance from the water's edge. A black and white tufted duck made little *currah currah* noises at them and the branches of the willow tree waved, although there was no breeze.

They looked around and took off their shoes and socks and rolled their trousers up to just below their knees. One of the men wiped his forehead and loosened his tie; then he took it off and folded it neatly on the bench. They walked down to the water and let it wash, cool and refreshing over their feet. Just one of them ventured underneath the bridge, while the other stayed where he was and continued to watch, up and down the river. A stone in the bridge jiggled around a bit and Chikitta saw her chance. While the men were occupied, she leapt from the tree to the bench where the zig zaggy tie was lying. She picked it up and sprang back, up to the top of the willow tree.

The first thing that one of the men noticed on returning to the bench was that his tie was missing.

"I know I left it here," he grunted. "It must be kids. If I find out who it is I'll giv'em what for."

Then, they walked back up the grassy slope, to the silver car, which was parked at the side of the road.

By the time the children returned to the bridge, the men had gone. Chikitta jumped down to meet them. She didn't take their hands as she usually did; instead, she kept them behind her back.

Soon, they were heading back up the river towards the muddy creek. They were too busy rowing and eating strawberry ice cream to notice that Chikitta was hiding underneath the seat. Suddenly, she sprang out and danced around in front of them. Donald and Jen looked at her in astonishment. Tied to her tail was a purple zig zaggy tie. It was folded into a beautiful billowing bow and hung just below her cheeky pink bottom.

***

Sleep was hard for Donald to come by that night. He must eventually have dropped off however because he could remember dreaming about two smartly dressed men and a little brown monkey that disappeared from a rabbit hutch. All that was left in her place was a purple zig zaggy tie.

He woke suddenly – something had disturbed him. There was a tinkering noise outside the caravan. His thoughts went first of all to the little black and white duck. The sound continued, like a tap tapping of a beak on the caravan door. He turned over and tried to get back to sleep, but then, he heard the sound of something being dropped. He sat up; that didn't sound like Tufty. He would have to take a look. What if someone was trying to get Chikitta.

He padded softly across to the door and pulled it open gently. The moon was not quite full and the sky was clear. As he peered outside, he could just make out the dark shadow of Chikitta, curled up in her hutch – she was safe at least. He could tell now that the clicks and taps were coming from the other side. He tip-toed, barefoot across the grass and stopped. There was a tall, dark shadow in front of him … he was sure it was the shadow that he'd seen once before – in the early morning gloom of the Big Top. It was stooped, this time over his unicycle and bits and pieces of tools were strewn across the ground. Donald was much closer to the figure today than he had been in the Big Top, but he still had no idea who it could be, or what he could be doing here, outside his caravan, in the middle of the night.

The Opening Show in Broadland

Things always seem brighter in the morning, even when the sky is grey and filled with rain. Donald was already beginning to wonder whether the ghostly figure of the previous night was purely in his imagination.

Jen was arriving shortly to take charge of Chikitta for the day as Donald had an important rehearsal. Tonight was the opening show of 'Signor Pepperino's Amazing Circus' and Donald was very excited. He had been working hard on his clown routine with Frankie and Tom and he felt confident. It was just a shame that Chikitta couldn't be included. His act with Victor Vulcan was also going well. He couldn't wait for Signor Pepperino to see him fly out of the canon to the high wire at the top of the Big Top.

He was meeting Victor Vulcan later on this afternoon, so he had the morning to check up on Chikitta. He wanted to make sure that she was collected and safely taken away from the circus.

Jen arrived on cue, just before breakfast. "Uncle Bob and I are going to the windmill for the day," she explained. "Chikitta will be safe there."

"The locked room might bring back some bad memories," said Donald.

"I'll let you know."

Chikitta jumped out of the hutch and took Jen's hand. Together they ran along the marshy track, over the broken stile, to the houseboat at the side of the river.

With Chikitta taken care of, Donald arrived early for his rehearsal. He was surprised to find that Victor Vulcan was already there. He smiled at Donald.

"How are you feeling?" he asked. "It's the big night tonight."

"A bit nervous, but not too bad."

"Good. Remember, you've nothing to worry about – you could do it blindfolded – now, there's a thought – maybe next time."

Donald shook his head. "I think I'd prefer to see where I'm going; especially at that speed."

Victor Vulcan put the canon in place and set the spring. "I've decided that we'll go for a slightly lower rope. Best to play it safe for the first time – save the high wire for the next show."

"But not the blindfold," added Donald.

They both laughed as they got ready to start the act.

At a given signal, Donald stepped inside the canon and streamlined his body into position. He looked up and through the opening and saw a red flag. At this point he started to count down in his head from ten.

'... 7,6,5 ...' he had the loop of the rope that he was aiming for in view '... 3,2,1 ...' the spring shot him forwards and he flew through the air. His position and timing was perfect and he reached the rope easily. He caught hold of it with both hands and was lowered to the ground.

"Bravo," said 'the Vulcan,' walking over. "Signor Pepperino will be very proud of you."

Donald beamed and got ready to take his position back inside the canon. He wanted to be absolutely sure that everything was right for this evening.

They repeated the stunt at least a dozen times before 'the Vulcan' was satisfied and then Donald went back to the caravan for a rest. Henry was waiting for him on the windowsill and immediately jumped down to nuzzle around his legs. Donald sat with Henry, purring on his lap, waiting for the show to start and for Chikitta to be returned to her hutch.

***

Jen arrived just in time to see Donald before the performance started. The circus was bustling with people coming to see the show.

"I've left Cheeky Keeta with Uncle Bob," she said – "there are too many people around now. As soon as the show starts and it's quiet, I'll bring her over."

"How was she at the windmill?"

"Fine. The new ticket man actually took her inside the locked room and she didn't mind at all."

"Good. Perhaps she's forgotten about getting kidnapped last year."

"Maybe, anyway, good luck for tonight. Are you nervous?"

"A bit, but I'm sure it'll be ok."

"You'll be brilliant. Uncle Bob has booked us up some tickets for one of the shows. I can't wait."

"It'll be even better by then. I'll actually be reaching the high wire – blindfolded."

"What!"

"Only joking. Anyway, I'll see you later."

Donald ran off to join Frankie and Tom who were waiting for him in the wings.

The music began. Unusually, the clown act was starting the show tonight. Victor Vulcan was to be the final act. Frankie and Tom jumped onto the trampoline, while Donald whizzed round on the unicycle. He counted his circuits before making for the ramp. His timing needed to be perfect. He circled the trampoline for the last time and then turned. Instantly, he knew that something wasn't right. He couldn't steer properly – the wheel seemed to be loosening in the frame. He'd be lucky to make it to the top of the ramp. He had to think quickly or he could end up in a heap on the floor. He sprang himself up from the seat and landed on his hands. In a desperate attempt to keep the act going, he cartwheeled up the ramp and onto the trampoline just as Tom was coming down. Then he caught hold of a swing and swung himself over to the other side and onto the stage next to Frankie and Tom.

The audience applauded. He'd managed it; no-one knew how close the act was to disaster.

"What were you playing at?" hissed Frankie as they ran off the stage. "That wasn't what we rehearsed."

"It's the unicycle – the wheel's come loose."

Signor Pepperino appeared at the wings with the unicycle, which he passed to Donald. "Well done Bambino, a good performance."

Tom bent down and spun the wheel. It wobbled and then fell onto the floor. "Gosh, I see what you mean. You did well to keep the act going."

Donald felt a sick feeling in his stomach as he thought of the dark figure outside his caravan. He pushed it from his mind. He still had an act to go.

At last it was time. The drums rolled as Signor Pepperino announced the guest appearance of Victor Vulcan.

The tall, striking figure of the great trapeze artist strode onto the stage to much applause. Then, to everyone's surprise, he stepped aside and held out his hand towards the wings. Donald ran onto the stage. At a given signal, he wormed his way into the canon and waited. It seemed like forever before the red flag waved; immediately the count down began.

'10, 9, 8 …' the looped rope was in view – just below the high wire, '7, 6, 5 …' he felt his heart miss a beat; the loop had disappeared. He needed to get 'the Vulcan's' attention; the spring was not set for the high wire and there was nothing else to grab hold of. Unfortunately, Victor Vulcan was concentrating on the lever. He hadn't noticed that the rope had gone. Donald smacked his fists desperately against the sides of the canon '… 3, 2, 1' – he was launched.

Twitch

All that Donald knew as he flew through the air was that the act was ruined. Hopefully, the nets would be there to catch him, but Signor Pepperino would be far from impressed and the audience would feel cheated; they'd come to see Victor Vulcan after all.

Suddenly, a rope from the opposite side of the Big Top's dome swung towards him. Once it was alongside, he grabbed it. He was jerked back across the arena and as he hung there, he was sure that he saw a brown tail disappear into the shadows.

From the dizzy height, Donald looked out for Victor Vulcan. He knew that he would be wondering why he was ending up on the opposite side of the stage. His eyes rested briefly on the cold, steely gaze. 'The Vulcan' was looking up; scowling at him.

Donald's landing came with much applause. Signor Pepperino looked astonished, but pleased. He held his arms out to Donald and presented him to the audience, who continued to cheer. Then, Victor Vulcan came to join them on the stage and the clapping grew louder. Donald looked nervously at the great man.

"It wasn't my fault," he whispered. "The rope disappeared; then another one flew out from nowhere." He decided not to mention the brown tail. Chikitta was still supposed to be missing after all.

They left the stage and to Donald's dismay, Victor Vulcan parted without a word.

"Ah, Bambino, many congratulations," said Signor Pepperino walking over. "It is unbelievable that you should fly out of the canon. I think I should be cross with you and with the great Victor Vulcan for letting you do it – but you did well." He patted Donald on the shoulder and then hurried off to see his other artists.

Donald felt uneasy. The two acts that he had been involved with had both nearly ended in disaster; perhaps he should have told Signor Pepperino. Instead, he walked back to his caravan.

Henry and Twitch were both there and seemed pleased to see him. Donald felt restless. He paced up and down for a bit; then he decided what he should do. He would go and see Victor Vulcan and talk to him again about the rope. He wanted to know whether he was still cross with him.

On his way to the brightly painted caravan, he was aware of something at his feet. It was Twitch. The little white rabbit had quite taken to following Donald around.

"Come on then," said Donald, stooping down to stroke him. "We'll go and face 'the Vulcan' together."

They arrived to find the door of the caravan not quite closed. Donald walked up the steps and knocked. There was no answer and so he tried again. He walked around the side and looked in all the windows, but there was no sign of anyone. He knew that he should wait, but already he could feel his confidence fading. He decided to go back.

"Come on Twitch; we'll try another time."

Suddenly, the little white rabbit shot up the steps, through Donald's legs and into the caravan.

"Twitch, come here," hissed Donald. "You can't just walk into other people's caravans."

Donald waited, but neither 'the Vulcan,' nor the rabbit appeared. There was only one thing for it. He would have to go in after him.

He pushed the door fully open and crept inside. He saw Twitch straight away. He was underneath the table, nibbling the cloth which hung over the sides. Donald crawled over to the rabbit.

"What's the matter? You'll get both of us into trouble if you're not careful."

Once the rabbit was safely in his arms, Donald crawled slowly backwards. He stood up … and caught sight of something lying on top of the table. It was a brown envelope and beside it was a piece of paper. He recognised the envelope straight away – and the map. He had seen it with Jen, underneath the bridge at Broadshaven. He wanted to get out quickly but could already hear someone on the steps outside. The huge form of Victor Vulcan framed the doorway as Donald and Twitch slipped behind a curtain. The door closed.

Inside Victor Vulcan's Caravan

Donald stood trembling behind the curtain. He could hear the rustling of papers and could see a large pair of brown shoes over by the table … which were suddenly coming his way. The curtains were thrust aside and there stood 'the Vulcan.' He glared at Donald.

"I … I'm sorry," Donald stammered. "I didn't mean to come in here; it was my rabbit; she bolted, so I came in after her."

"It seems that you have very little control over your animals." 'The Vulcan' looked slightly less annoyed.

Donald nodded, remembering the fuss that Henry had made last time he was here, not to mention Chikitta and the trifle.

"I came to talk to you about the show," continued Donald, "but you weren't here and …" Donald glanced over to the table. The envelope and the piece of paper had gone. He couldn't help feeling that the map somehow connected 'the Vulcan' to the two men. He wondered how much he should say. He decided to mention the rope, but not the loose wheel – at least not for the time being.

"It was during the count down that I noticed it," he began. "I had my eye on the rope and suddenly it disappeared. I didn't know what I was going to grab hold of and I couldn't get your attention."

"So what exactly happened?" asked 'the Vulcan,' leaning closer. "Where did the other rope come from?"

"I've no idea," said Donald, not quite truthfully. He'd seen the brown tail and was sure that Chikitta had somehow released it for him.

"I see." 'The Vulcan' got up. Donald looked at the great big man, with his strong, muscular arms and his thick sweep of dark brown hair. He hadn't meant to upset him.

Then he smiled at Donald. "Well, I suppose I should congratulate you for saving the act."

Donald felt relieved. It seemed that 'the Vulcan' understood after all.

Suddenly, there was a tap at the caravan door and in padded a little black and white crested duck.

"Tufty," gasped Donald. "What are you doing here?"

"Another one of your animals?" asked 'the Vulcan,' sarcastically.

Donald quickly scooped the duck up with his spare arm and made a rapid exit.

Chikitta was in the hutch when he arrived back. She was poking pieces of straw through the wire at a creamy tipped tail. Tufty flapped out of Donald's arms and Henry shot off the hutch, to the top of the caravan. Chikitta scowled at them.

Donald gave the monkey a pat on the head. "Thanks Chikitta. If it wasn't for you, the act would have been ruined."

It had been a long day. Donald left the rabbit hutch, and then went into his caravan – to bed. Henry and Twitch curled up together on the windowsill and Tufty flew over the marshy track and the broken stile, and nestled for the night amongst the reeds of the muddy creek.

Charlie and Josh

Donald woke feeling excited. Charlie and Josh were arriving today to join Jen and her Uncle Bob for a holiday on the houseboat. They had spent last summer on the broads with their parents. This year, they were allowed to come on their own, under the supervision of the ferryman. Donald thought happily of the camp they had made, as well as the adventures that they had enjoyed together. He would take Chikitta down to the river straight after breakfast.

The circus was busy, so Donald had Chikitta in a bag, which was slung over his shoulder. The bag wriggled about a bit, but he hoped that no-one would notice. To his surprise, he arrived to find that Charlie and Josh were already there. Chikitta jumped out of the bag and into the trees. Soon all kinds of missiles were coming their way. Josh looked up just as a pine cone landed on his nose.

"Chikitta," he said happily, "we've missed you. Where have you been?"

"I haven't had time to tell you yet," said Jen. "We have to keep her hidden. She's a wanted monkey."

"What! I know she can be a bit of a nuisance but …"

"It's true," continued Donald. "She's upset these two men. They want the ferryman to give up his mooring, but he won't sell. Unfortunately, they won't take no for an answer."

"But what has it got to do with Chikitta?"

"She grabbed a tie and swung it round the man's neck," explained Donald. "He said that she tried to strangle him."

"It sounds like he deserved it," said Charlie."

"Anyway, they've reported her to the police. As soon as they find her, they're going to hand her over."

"Except that they're not going to find her," said Jen firmly.

"Where are you hiding her?" asked Josh.

"That's the clever bit," grinned Donald. "She's in my rabbit hutch. You haven't met Twitch yet. You'll like him."

"And how does Twitch feel about it?" asked Josh, looking amused. "Not a very peaceful housemate."

"Oh, don't worry about Twitch. He's in my caravan for the time being."

"Gosh; things are never dull around here," said Charlie, "not with Chikitta around."

"That's not all." Donald turned to Jen. "She saved the show last night."

"What do you mean? I put her in the hutch just after the performance started."

"Well she didn't stay there. Both of my acts were nearly ruined. The wheel on my unicycle came loose while I was doing the clown routine, and then, the rope that I was supposed to grab hold of after I'd been catapulted out of the canon simply disappeared. If it hadn't been for Chikitta throwing me another one, I'd have fallen into the net. The act would have been a complete flop."

"Good old Cheeky Keeta."

Jen turned to Charlie and Josh. "Donald's performing with the famous Victor

Vulcan. It's been a secret. Even Signor Pepperino doesn't know anything about it."

"Well he does now, but I haven't told him that it nearly all ended in disaster. Actually, there's something else," said Donald, looking more serious.

"What as well as Chikitta being virtually under arrest, a broken unicycle and you coming out of an exploding canon with nowhere to go … what else could there be?" Charlie shook his head at Josh, who looked equally baffled.

"Jen and I went to the bridge at Broadshaven," he began to explain. "We found this secret place, behind one of the stones underneath the arch."

"There was a brown envelope inside," continued Jen, "with a map – of the circus site and the moorings at the muddy creek. We saw those two awful men hanging around too – the men that want to arrest Chikitta."

"Then, when we went back the next day, the map was gone."

"Did the men take it?"

"We never saw them, but it must have been them. Chikitta pinched one of their ties."

"Now I'm completely confused," said Charlie. "I think I detect another Broadland mystery coming on."

"I don't think it was the two men that took the map," said Donald.

Jen looked round in surprise. "Why ever not? They must have been there."

"Because I've seen it since … in Victor Vulcan's caravan. I went there yesterday, with Twitch, to talk to him about the rope disappearing. He wasn't in and I was just about to leave, when Twitch shot inside – he wouldn't come out, so, I had to go in after him."

"Then what happened," asked Jen impatiently. "What about the map?"

"It was there; in his caravan; lying on the table."

"But what would Victor Vulcan be doing with it? And what about the other two – 'Stripy'and 'Spotty'?"

"Perhaps they left it for him… there's one more thing."

"Go on," said Jen.

"Last week, I went to the Big Top early to practise. The shutters were down and it was dark inside; I could hear someone moving around at the side of the stage, but I couldn't tell who it was. Then, two nights ago, I saw someone outside my caravan – it was too dark to see them clearly, but they were messing around with my unicycle and … I'm sure it was the same person; someone big."

"Surely you don't think it was Victor Vulcan," said Jen.

Donald could feel his cheeks burning. He didn't want to think that. He shook his head. "Why would he want to wreck his own act? We spent hours practising."

"Maybe he wants to ruin the circus. Maybe he wants to help those two men get the land and the moorings."

"Maybe the circus is in the way," added Josh. "Everyone wants to see 'Signor Pepperino's Amazing Circus' in the summer – including us."

94

"Have you mentioned any of this to Signor Pepperino or the ferryman?" asked Charlie.

"They know that we're hiding Chikitta," Donald replied, "but they don't know where."

"Don't worry. We won't mention a thing."

"What now?" asked Charlie.

They looked at each other, waiting for someone to make a suggestion.

"I think we should go back to the bridge," said Jen at last. "That's where the mystery started. Perhaps that's where it'll be solved."

No-one had a better idea. Charlie and Josh helped the ferryman with the picnic, while Donald and Jen sought out the life jackets and untied the boat. Before long, the four of them, and Chikitta, were rowing down the river, towards the bridge at Broadshaven.

Marsh End

There was less activity on the grassy bank today. The rain had stopped at last but the sky was still overcast and the silver grey water appeared less inviting. Once the boat was moored, Jen led the way across the familiar grassy slope, to the ledge, underneath the bridge. Chikitta was soon hidden amongst the drooping fronds of the willow tree.

Donald removed the stone. The others watched eagerly as he put his hand inside.

"I can feel something," he said excitedly.

They crowded round as he pulled out a cardboard tube. Inside was a rolled up piece of paper. Donald, grateful for the pale green curtain of willow leaves, pulled the scroll open.

"Look, here's the circus site again. It looks different."

"It's split into six parts," said Jen, leaning over. "They could be houses."

"There's another drawing underneath," said Donald. "It must be the moorings, at the muddy creek; there are six of them."

"This one's Uncle Bob's."

"So, we've got six houses," said Donald, "each with their own mooring. That could make someone a lot of money."

"But why would someone leave it here?" asked Charlie.

"Because Victor Vulcan doesn't want anyone to know he's involved," said Jen. "He wouldn't want Signor Pepperino to find out that his famous new trapeze artist is trying to ruin his circus."

"What are we going to do?" asked Josh.

"We could take the map to show Signor Pepperino," suggested Donald.

"But it doesn't belong to us," said Josh.

Jen raised her eyebrows and Charlie and Josh turned red. They could all remember how the two boys had taken the ferryman's boat last year, even though it didn't belong to them.

"That's settled then." Jen replaced the stone and put the cardboard tube, along with the scroll in her bag. They decided to eat their lunch away from the river, on a bench – far enough away from their secret hiding place, but close enough to keep an eye on Chikitta.

The lunch was as generous as ever. The ferryman believed in food being simple but wholesome. The bread was fresh and chunky, perfectly matching the large slabs of cheese and thick slices of ham. As usual, there was plenty. Once lunch was over, they continued to pass the time watching the boats motoring under the bridge. Donald particularly enjoyed watching the sailing boats as they had tall masts, which had to be taken down before they could get through the arch. He watched as a navy blue motor boat went through and waited for it to appear on the other side. The river remained clear.

"That's strange," he said. "Where's the blue boat gone?"

"Can't say I noticed," said Jen.

"I saw it go underneath the bridge, but it hasn't come out."

"There it is," said Josh, pointing.

Sure enough, the navy launch was reversing back up the river. A familiar figure climbed out, onto the bank; then he disappeared back underneath the bridge.

"It's Victor Vulcan," whispered Jen. "I bet he's gone to get the scroll."

The children quickly packed up the picnic bag and ran further up the slope. They watched anxiously as a branch of the willow tree waved up and down, and a tail swung from side to side, just above the old stone bridge.

"If he spots Chikitta, we're in big trouble," said Donald.

A tall, frowning figure appeared again. He seemed agitated and was looking up and down the river; then, he got back into the navy blue boat and continued upstream.

"Come on," said Jen, running towards the rowing boat. "Let's follow him."

"You must be joking," said Charlie, "he doesn't look very happy."

She took no notice. Once on the boat, she handed Charlie the oars and he reluctantly started to row up the river, in the wake of the navy blue launch.

"You two will have to do the rowing," said Jen. "He won't recognise either of you."

Charlie realised that there was no point in arguing. He knew that Jen could be very determined when she wanted to be.

They soon lost sight of the motor boat. No amount of encouragement from Jen could persuade Charlie to row any faster.

"Hey, what about Chikitta?" said Josh.

Donald and Jen looked at each other.

"We'll have to go back," said Donald.

"No we won't," said Jen. "Chikitta can look after herself. We'll collect her on our way home."

"She didn't do a very good job looking after herself last year," grumbled Charlie, as he pulled on the oars.

"Keep going," said Jen, "he can't have got far."

The little wooden rowing boat continued its way up the river. Donald enjoyed looking at all the huts and chalets; lodges and boat docks which flanked either side of the river.

People were sitting on wooden decks, playing with their boats and tending their pot plants and hanging baskets. The next dock along caught his attention.

"There's the motor boat. Victor Vulcan must be in there."

They continued rowing past the chalet. The cedar tiles were painted brown and a wooden deck ran past the front door. There was a trellis, covered in creeper, which provided a convenient screen from passing boats, making it hard for the children to see what was going on. They did however notice that there was a shed to one side of the front door, and a porch on the other.

Jen signalled to Charlie to keep rowing. She checked the name and number as they drifted past – 'Marsh End, 88.' It seemed well named. It was one of the last chalets on this side of the river; from here, there stretched marshland as far as you could see. There was a dyke at the edge of the marsh, and beyond, cattle grazed.

It was just a short way up the river, in front of a disused windmill, that they found a place to moor. They left the boat and followed an overgrown track, which took them past the backs of the chalets – back towards number 88.

"You stay here," said Donald to Charlie and Josh as he undid the gate. "Jen and I will take a look inside."

Charlie and Josh seemed very happy with this idea and stood smartly to attention, either side of the gate.

Donald and Jen crept round to the front of the chalet. There was a window underneath the porch which looked into one of the rooms. They could see a desk running across one of the walls.

"It looks like some sort of office," whispered Jen.

"It could be; let's try the other side." Donald started to crawl along the trellised deck to another, larger window, next to the front door. They peered inside.

"That's him," said Donald. "He doesn't look very happy."

Victor Vulcan was on the phone, pacing up and down the room. His raised voice could be heard through the flimsy cedar walls.

"I expect 'Spotty' and 'Stripy' are getting told off for not leaving the drawings under the bridge."

"Well they won't get any sympathy from me," said Jen.

They saw the figure move towards the window and then the front door opened. Donald and Jen quickly scurried back across the deck.

'The Vulcan' walked round the side of the chalet to the shed. They could hear him rummaging around a bit before returning. He put some keys on a hook by the front door, then left.

The children scrambled to their feet and ran to the gate. Charlie and Josh were still smartly positioned on the other side.

"He's gone," said Donald. "We can have a proper look round now."

"Do we have to?" asked Charlie.

Donald and Jen had already gone. Donald went straight to the shed, while Jen tried the front door. Both were locked.

"The key to this padlock is just inside the front door," said Donald. "I saw him put it there."

"That's a shame. There's no way we can get through a locked door."

"There's one window open at the back," said Josh helpfully, "but it's tiny."

They wandered about a bit, wondering what to do. They couldn't even look through the windows any more as the blinds had now been pulled down. 'The Vulcan' had seen to that just before he had left.

Charlie and Josh sat down on the patch of grass at the front of the chalet.

"We've missed the tide," said Jen, walking over. "Rowing will be hard work on the way back."

A familiar *currah currah* noise caught their attention.

"Tufty," shouted Donald, jumping up.

The black and white duck, with a speckly grey crest was dabbing its way towards them. It splashed out of the water and waddled over.

Donald could already feel the idea buzzing around in his head. "Tufty, I want you to do something for me."

The duck pecked at Donald's feet.

"I want you to get Chikitta."

The others looked at him in surprise.

"A small monkey might get through the window. I want to take a look inside that shed. Something's still puzzling me."

"And the answer's in the shed?" said Charlie doubtfully.

Donald watched Tufty fall back into the water. He knew that it wouldn't take the duck long to reach the bridge … but would he bring Chikitta? He lay back on the warm, soft grass … and waited.

The Shed

Two men emerged from the berries and brambles of the marshy track. A green spotty tie hung neatly in front of a crisp white shirt and a pair of shiny black shoes skidded around in the mud. The other man wore a plain, turquoise tie; the purple zig zaggy one had disappeared as mysteriously as had the drawings from underneath the bridge. He kicked a foot full of sticks and stones into the water, in the direction of a swan that happened to be gliding past.

"Great big brutes; don't want them getting too close."

The swan displayed a majestic arc of white feathers and then continued on its way. The man breathed a sigh of relief and loosened the turquoise knot a little. "If it's not monkeys, it's bloomin' swans. The sooner we get away from this place the better."

The man with the spotty tie flapped a piece of paper at him. "Just as soon as the job's done. Look, here comes the old fool now."

They turned the smiles on like a switch as the ferryman came onto the deck. He didn't look pleased to see them.

The man with the turquoise tie walked over. He kept his hand protectively round his neck and glanced up into the trees. He was sure that the flea ridden monkey was around here somewhere.

"We've come to be of assistance," he began, raising his eyebrows sympathetically – still smiling.

The ferryman stared back, blankly.

"It's about the mooring posts," he continued. "We've another mooring reserved for you. You can take possession of it as soon as you agree to sell this muddy patch."

He tried to scrape some of the mud from his shoes on a nearby tree root. He found that as fast as one shoe was scraped clean, the other became submerged in the slippery brown stuff. He'd be glad to get away from this dreary, overgrown patch of slime.

"If you don't sign, I'm afraid we'll have to let the mooring go. Our only wish is to help."

The ferryman hadn't moved. His face was stony and his hands shook as he took the piece of paper. Without a word, he tore it into a great many pieces and returned to his cabin. The wooden shutters closed with a bang.

The two men were left with mud still on their shoes, and the smiles wiped from their faces.

"Now what?" fumed the man with the spotty tie.

The other man kicked some more grit and stones into the creek as another swan ambled by. "Come on. We'll pay a visit to Marsh End. If someone's been snooping around Broadshaven Bridge and taken our drawings, we need to check Wally's place. Wouldn't do for things to get into the wrong hands."

"He won't like that. You know how he hates people interfering."

"Wally won't know, and he'll be as upset as us if it all goes 'pear shaped' – he stands to make a lot of money from our little development."

The two men slipped and skidded their way back over the broken stile, along the marshy track, past the circus, to the silver car, which took them to Broadshaven Bridge. From there, they followed the footpath, which ran along behind the chalets, to the one which was right at the end – to number 88, to Marsh End.

***

"Here he comes," shouted Donald excitedly.

The others had become bored waiting, but Donald had been sure that Tufty would return.

"What about Cheeky Keeta?" asked Jen.

"No sign … yet …"

All eyes were on the duck as he flapped out of the water and made his soft *currah currah* noises at them. The furry brown torpedo that landed on the grass next to them took them all by surprise.

"Chikitta," said Donald happily. "I knew you'd come. Good old Tufty."

Chikitta instantly turned her back on the black and white duck.

"Oh don't start sulking again. We need you to do something for us."

The monkey took Donald's hand, and together, they walked round to the back of the chalet.

"Look," said Donald, pointing at the window. "We need you to get through there." Then he walked back round to the front of the building, and poked his finger inside the keyhole, swivelling it one way and then the other.

"Fetch us the keys Chiktta – quick."

Without hesitation, Chikitta ran to the back window and with one of her supersonic springs, she sprang straight inside. She was at the front door in no time, where she collected the keys from the hook and then returned to the waiting children.

"Hurray. Good old Cheeky Keeta."

Chikitta bowed and curtsied as if she was performing on the Big Top stage.

"That's enough," said Donald, more seriously. "You still need to keep hidden. Charlie and Josh can keep watch again outside the gate … Jen and I are going to take a look inside that shed."

Tufty Gets His Revenge

There was nothing extraordinary to catch Donald's attention on entering the shed. His first impression was that it was uncluttered and tidy. A lawn mower rested against one wall and behind it there were a number of gardening tools. Above his head were wooden planks which served as a platform to store oars and paddles. On the other side was a canoe.

"Not much to go on," said Jen. "Let's go; we've still got the drawings to show Signor Pepperino."

"But I want proof that Victor Vulcan is involved. It'll be here – somewhere."

Donald continued walking up and down. He knew that Jen was impatient to go – they shouldn't be in here and they had a difficult row back; against the tide. There was a bag hanging over the canoe. It seemed to be full of old rags and on the top lay a pair of gardening gloves. He heard Jen sigh as he took the bag from the nail and then tipped everything out, onto the floor. The contents spilled into an unlikely looking bundle of junk.

"I told you; I really think …"

She stopped as Donald picked up one of the old rags from the bottom of the pile – except that it wasn't a rag at all. It was a wig. The hair was thick and dark brown.

"I think Victor Vulcan must wear a wig," said Donald.

"How come? He had a fine head of brown hair when he left just now."

"I don't know, perhaps it's a spare one." Donald stuffed it into Jen's bag with the scroll and continued fingering through all the other scraps of cloth. A slightly crumpled piece of paper fell from amongst the pile. He spread out the creases and began to read – 'Payment of £50.00 made to Wallace Stubbs; balance of £50,000.00 to be paid on completion of the purchase of Hickling Estate and the Catfield Dyke moorings.' It was signed, Oliver Burns and George Ashcroft Developers Ltd.

"I don't think our special trapeze artist is Victor Vulcan at all," said Donald. "His name is Wallace Stubbs."

"But what about the canon act? You have to be an acrobat to do something like that."

"Except that he hasn't done anything yet. It's me that has flown out of the canon remember. I've not seen him perform once, and I bet Signor Pepperino hasn't either."

"So he's helping those two developers buy the circus site."

"By ruining everything and getting a quick sale. We'll take this too," said Donald, adding the piece of paper to the bag.

"Shh, I think I heard something."

Chikitta was chattering and jumping around excitedly, and there were strange whistling and tweeting noises coming from behind the gate.

"That'll be Charlie and Josh; someone's coming."

Donald quickly swept up the contents from the floor into the bag, and hung it back on the nail. Then he locked the door and gave the keys to Chikitta. She knew what she had to do with them.

Chikitta leapt back out of the window and into the trees just as two men walked through the gate.

Donald and Jen ran across the grass and slipped into the water. They swam round to the boat dock and grabbed a piece of rope which was trailing in the water from one of the metal mooring posts.

"I hope Charlie and Josh have kept hidden," whispered Jen.

"And Chikitta. If they see her, it'll give the game away."

***

"Everything seems in order," said one of the men, smoothing his spotty tie down in front of his pristine white cotton shirt. "I told you there was nothing to worry about."

"There's a window open. That's plain careless," grumbled his friend.

"You'd have to be tiny to fit through there."

"All the same, no point in taking chances."

The man with the turquoise tie pulled a dustbin over so that it was directly underneath the open window. He climbed on top of it, put his hand through the opening and somehow managed to slam it shut.

"There, that should do it."

They wandered round to the front and checked the chalet door … and then the shed. Confident that no-one had been inside, they walked out onto the grass. They stood next to the water and looked up and down the river.

Donald and Jen had squeezed themselves as far back into the boat dock as they could.

Suddenly, there was a rustle in the trees and a handful of soggy, furry catkins flew out, towards the two smartly dressed men. They landed with a plop on the two, slightly balding targets.

"Yuk. Some filthy little bird has gone and done his business on top of my head."

"Yeah, mine too – what I'd give to strangle the lot of 'em."

"We'd best wash it off."

They walked round to the dock area, where there was a gently sloping ramp into the water.

"Oh no," whispered Donald. "They're coming this way."

"So are Charlie and Josh," said Jen, pointing out into the river. "Look; they've got the rowing boat."

Donald and Jen immediately disappeared under the water and reappeared at the far side of the rowing boat.

"Quick," said Donald, gasping, "wait for us to get in and then start rowing back down the river."

"What about the bag?" said Jen. "I left it on the side of the dock so it wouldn't get wet."

"Oh no, I forgot the bag; all our evidence is in there."

Donald and Jen managed to hook their legs over the boat and fall into the bottom as Charlie rowed. They were suddenly met by a *currah curah* sound.

"Tufty; youre just the duck we need." Donald pointed to the bag which was still lying on the side of the dock.

"Tell Chikitta … bring it here."

The duck obediently waddled across the grass and past the two men, who still had their heads dipped in the water. Then he flapped around the bag a bit, and made a raucous growling sound which echoed out and into the trees overhead. It seemed to do the trick. Chikitta jumped onto the roof of the chalet, where she watched the duck perform a weird little dance across a bag which was lying at the edge of the dock. She sprang down and grabbed it from underneath Tufty's webbed feet.

The startled duck squawked up into the air and flew over two men who were bent down at the side of the river. In a complete state of panic, he released his droppings, just as the two balding heads lifted from the water.

"That duck's just poohed all over your head – again!" said the man with the green spotty tie.

"And yours. It must have something wrong with it."

"There's something wrong with it alright. Come on; I'm going."

The two men dipped their heads once more into the river and then made a quick escape along the footpath, to the silver car, which was parked just by the bridge at Broadshaven.

Some Bad News for Donald

Josh was now rowing and they were making good progress. Although the tide was running out, it had steadied; pieces of grass and the occasional feather were floating past quite slowly.

"We must reach Uncle Bob before those two men get him to sign anything," said Jen.

"And I want to see Signor Pepperino," Donald added. "The sooner he realises that Victor Vulcan is a fake, the better."

"Wallace Stubbs you mean."

"Charlie looked at Josh. "Is someone going to tell us what this is all about?"

"We've found a wig," explained Jen. "It looks just like Victor Vulcan's hair … and there's a letter, written to Wallace Stubbs; it proves that he's involved with those two men."

"And you found all that out in the shed?" said Charlie, looking impressed.

Donald nodded. "Couldn't have done it without Chikitta and Tufty though. She snatched the bag, right out from under their noses."

"What about Tufty?"

"He made a lot of flapping and squawking noises."

They all laughed and Jen took her place at the oars. She cut them cleanly through the water. She was determined to get back before dark.

***

When they eventually arrived at the muddy creek, they were pleased to see that Signor Pepperino and the ferryman were sitting on the houseboat together. Donald noticed that they both looked very serious.

Signor Pepperino met them at the water's edge and took the rope. He secured it to the tree and led the children onto the deck of the houseboat.

"Well I must say Bambino, I'm relieved to see you back. We expected you hours ago."

The ferryman looked at his niece. "I warned you about the tides," he said disapprovingly.

"It was my fault," said Donald. "Jen wanted to come back earlier. I um … had a job to do."

Signor Pepperino raised his eyebrows. "Ah Bambino, it seems that we all have jobs to do. Bob here is in danger of losing his home at the creek, and we have troubles of our own, back at the circus."

"What kind of troubles?" asked Donald.

"Victor Vulcan has been kind enough to inform me of some safety hazards that need addressing. He also told me about your near disasters Bambino and has advised me to shut down for a few weeks to sort things out."

"But people have brought tickets."

Signor Pepperino shook his head. "That's too bad Bambino. I cannot permit my trapeze artists and acrobats to take risks; I have decided to take his advice. 'Signor Pepperino's Amazing Circus' will not operate for at least two weeks. I just hope that it won't prevent us coming back next year."

"Which would suit Victor Vulcan fine," said Jen indignantly.

The ferryman looked up in surprise. "And what's that supposed to mean?"

"There are things you should know," she continued, "about Victor Vulcan and those two men; they're crooks."

"I think you'd better explain," said Signor Pepperino, getting up for the bottle of elderberry juice. He poured each of them a glass.

"We found this," said Jen, pulling the scroll from her bag. "See, down here is the muddy creek. They want the moorings for their new houses."

"Which they intend to build on the circus site," added Donald.

"This is very interesting," said Signor Pepperino, "but it doesn't mean that anything dishonest is going on – and what has it all to do with Victor Vulcan?"

"Wallace Stubbs you mean," said Jen, holding out the wig.

"Show Signor Pepperino the letter."

The ferryman and Signor Pepperino looked gravely over the bits and pieces of information that the children had somehow produced from the bag.

"So they want to discredit my circus," said Signor Pepperino, frowning.

"Then, once they have the moorings, they're set to make big profit," added the ferryman. "They've been putting the pressure on recently; been down to see me at least three times in the past two days. Said if I don't sell, I'll miss out on a mooring altogether."

Chikitta chose this moment to join them. A lot of fuss had been made of her on the way back and she was feeling very pleased with herself. She jumped into the galley and started juggling a few plates.

"That monkey," said Signor Pepperino. "I forgot – there's another problem we need to sort out."

"Cheeky Keeta's not a problem," said Jen indignantly. "We wouldn't have discovered anything without her help. She's a star."

Chikitta turned round and waved a cheeky pink bottom in their faces; then she leapt back up into the trees.

There was another noise coming from the marshy track and a tall figure came towards them. Victor Vulcan greeted them from the side of the river. "I thought I might find you here," he said, looking at the ringmaster. "I've done as we agreed; cancelled all future shows."

"I thought we agreed two weeks," said Signor Peperino.

Victor Vulcan shrugged. "Thought it better to play it safe."

"But, but …" Donald desperately tried to catch the great ringmaster's attention. "I thought …"

"That'll be all," said Signor Pepperino briskly. "You heard 'the Vulcan' and it's getting late. Time we all went home."

Signor Pepperino walked on ahead with Victor Vulcan. Donald lingered a little longer, until they had disappeared over the broken stile. He had a scroll, a wig and a letter to take care of, as well as a mischievous monkey who needed to be returned to the rabbit hutch.

A Very Special Performance at Broadland

The blinds were down and a 'Do Not Disturb' sign hung on the door of Signor Pepperino's caravan. The circus lacked the usual hustle and bustle and as Donald wandered in and out of marquees, and trod the familiar paths around the

caravans, he felt strangely alone. It was as if the circus had already ceased to exist. He needed to talk some more to Signor

Pepperino, but the great ringmaster did not seem to want to see him. He decided to go back to check up on Chikitta.

Henry was waiting on the windowsill and he immediately ran over, purring and rubbing his head against Donald's legs.

Someone else was there to meet him. Victor Vulcan was smiling broadly and Donald could already feel Henry bristling between his ankles.

"A bad business," he said, still smiling. "Circus could be closed for a month at least."

"Not if I can help it" said Donald, scowling.

"What do you mean?" asked Victor Vulcan, the smile suddenly fading.

"Oh nothing; I just think we might be over reacting."

"Can never be too careful," said 'the Vulcan,' perking up again. "By the way, any sign of that monkey?"

Donald saw his gaze shift towards the caravan; at the same time, there were some rustling sounds, which seemed to come from the hutch.

'Not now Chikitta,' he thought anxiously.

But it was Henry who had caught Victor Vulcan's attention. The cat had moved away from Donald and was circling round 'the Vulcan's' ankles, with his tail waving and his fur prickling. One menacing hiss was enough to encourage the great trapeze artist to make a hasty retreat back to his own caravan.

"Well done," said Donald, bending down to stroke the still prickly fur. "That told him." Then he wandered back inside his caravan and wondered whatever he was going to do with the rest of his day.

A scraping sound dusted the silence and Twitch hopped over to where a piece of paper lay; it had been pushed underneath the door. Donald ran over and picked it up. He wondered whether it would be another map. It wasn't. There was a message, signed with a top hat. It was from Signor Pepperino.

> 'Signor Pepperino's Amazing Circus' will be performing tonight. Have your acts ready and be prepared for a surprise.

Donald felt relieved. Signor Pepperino was not taken in by Victor Vulcan. The note was a secret – Victor Vulcan must not know.

Donald immediately felt much better. He was soon running with Chikitta, along the marshy track, over the broken stile, to the houseboat at the side of the water. Jen had spotted him and was waving something in her hand.

"We're all coming to the show tonight," she said excitedly. "Uncle Bob's got us tickets."

"How did you know it was back on?"

"Signor Pepperino's been to see us. He says that he's got a busy day ahead of him – he's getting the circus 'ship shape' and ready for a very special act. Are you flying out of the canon again?"

Donald shook his head. "Victor Vulcan doesn't know that we're opening. It's a secret; I'll just be doing my clown routine."

"Shame, I was looking forward to you blasting out across the Big Top."

"So were we," said Charlie, "but I bet it'll still be amazing."

"What about your unicycle?" said Josh. "Have you mended that wobbly wheel?"

"Signor Pepperino has taken care of it. It's locked up inside his caravan."

"Well don't worry about Cheeky Keeta; we'll take care of her."

"Thanks; I guess I'd better be going."

Donald waved to his friends and hurried back, over the broken stile, along the marshy track, to the circus.

***

There was a curious, simmering bubble of expectancy that evening. A hushed secrecy had swept the circus and this only increased everyone's excitement. No-one had mentioned the show to Victor Vulcan; only Donald knew why.

There were ten minutes to go and the performers were in position. Signor Pepperino looked particularly dashing. His top hat shone and his black shoes gleamed. He cast a reassuring smile at Donald and his blue eyes twinkled.

Suddenly, a tall, dark figure strode angrily into the Big Top. He stood facing the great ringmaster, glaring.

"What's all this about?" he growled. "We agreed that the circus would remain closed until all the problems were sorted out."

"And indeed they are all sorted out," said Signor Pepperino. "Now, please come with me. I have a special seat reserved for you – as our most distinguished guest."

Donald watched as a very confused looking Victor Vulcan was ushered to a seat at the front of the arena. At the same time, two other men were being shown into the next two seats. They looked equally bewildered.

"What are you doing here?" hissed 'the Vulcan.'

"We might well ask you the same thing. We got an invitation from your Signor Pepperino," said the man with the spotty tie. "Said he wanted to discuss business."

"I thought you'd got the circus shut down," said the man with the turquoise tie.

"So did I," mumbled Victor Vulcan. "I'm not sure what this is all about, but I don't like it one little bit."

Suddenly the music started up and the lights dimmed. The show began. Signor Pepperino introduced each act in flamboyant style. Three people sat in the front row, stony faced and with their arms firmly folded. At last it was time for the clowns.

Donald pedalled into the ring, circling the trampoline. He shot up the ramp, flew over the top, just as Tom began his somersault. Chikitta took him completely by surprise. She appeared at the end of a rope, weaving in and out of Frankie and Tom, before landing on Donald's shoulder, and onto the Big Top stage.

Everyone applauded and Signor Pepperino held his hands out to the three clowns and to Chikitta, who got more cheers than anyone. Her next trick seemed to even take Signor Pepperino by surprise. She jumped down to the front of the stage, and waved a cheeky pink bottom in front of three men sitting in the front row. Tied to her tail, was a purple, zig zaggy tie.

The man with the turquoise tie looked as if he was about to explode and his face turned its own delicate shade of purple.

Her next trick was to snatch at Victor Vulcan's head of thick brown hair. The wig came away easily in her hands.

"And now," said the great ringmaster, beaming at the audience, "I would like to present you with, the genuine … Victor Vulcan."

A familiar looking figure ran onto the stage. His thick, dark hair very much resembled the 'Victor Vulcan' sitting in the front row, though he stood slightly shorter. He smiled warmly at Donald.

'So that's the real Victor Vulcan,' thought Donald. He watched as the real trapeze artist climbed into the canon. In seconds, 'the Vulcan' was flying towards the high wire at a phenomenal speed. By the time he landed back on the stage, he had completed a sizzling sequence of spins and somersaults.

Donald joined in the applause as he looked up at the great trapeze artist. Then, another canon was wheeled in. Donald suddenly found himself being picked up into the air and placed inside.

"Count back from ten and make for the high wire," whispered 'the Vulcan.'

A red flag appeared and Donald began to count, '… 8,7,6 …' he had the wire in view, '… 4,3,2 …' Suddenly, Victor Vulcan shot out of the other canon, '… 1, 0 …'

Donald flew out of his canon, towards the high wire.

As he grabbed hold of it, he was aware that Victor Vulcan was directly above him and making towards the other side of the arena. He twisted and turned down the rope, to the Big Top stage and Donald was gradually lowered down onto the floor next to him. Donald could feel his cheeks glowing with pride as Victor Vulcan picked him up and onto his shoulders, while the crowd stood up and cheered. Signor Pepperino looked at him and beamed.

"Ah, Bambino," he said. "One day you too will be a world famous trapeze artist."

From the top of Victor Vulcan's shoulders, Donald looked round for Jen, but it was the three men in the front row who were making for the exit that caught his eye. He heard a slight scuffle amongst all the applause, and then they disappeared.

Tufty's Surprise

Donald was quickly whisked off the stage to the great ringmaster's caravan, where there was already quite a party of people gathered inside.

"Great canon act," said Charlie grinning. "You kept that pretty quiet."

"That's because I didn't know anything about it."

"And what about Cheeky Keeta? I thought she was supposed to stay hidden."

Donald shrugged. "I didn't know anything about that either."

Signor Pepperino walked over to Donald and put his arm around his shoulders. "Ah Bambino, I'm sorry to have kept things from you, but it was important that Mr Wallace Bragg and his two accomplices didn't find out that the real Victor Vulcan was coming to Broadland. I contacted him just as soon as I discovered that our so called trapeze artist was a fake – thanks to you Bambino."

"However did you find Him?"

"Ah, it wasn't difficult Bambino. I guessed that he was probably touring far away from here. Wallace Bragg wouldn't want to run the risk of bumping into the real Victor Vulcan."

"I see what you mean."

"So, he cut short his Scandinavian tour just as soon as he found out what that scoundrel was up to. I presume you still have the scroll and the letter."

Donald nodded – "and a wig."

Signor Pepperino chuckled. "Good, I know someone who will be very pleased to see all the evidence."

It was at this point that Donald noticed the person standing by the door. He recognised him straight away – it was the patrol man who they had helped last summer to solve the mystery at the windmill.

"So the river detectives have been busy once again," he said smiling. "Thanks to you, the circus is safe, not to mention the moorings at the muddy creek."

Donald looked at the ferryman. He seemed a lot happier now. "What about

Chikitta?" Donald asked. "Is she still a 'wanted monkey'?"

The patrol man laughed. "Certainly not; in fact I have something for her."

He took something from his pocket. To Donald's surprise, it was the purple zig zaggy tie, which had a golden medal hanging from it. He placed it round the monkey's neck.

"There we are… the highest honour that can be awarded to a monkey."

Chikitta took the medal in her hands and jumped around the caravan screeching and swinging from curtain to curtain. As usual, she was making the most of being the centre of attention.

"Now, I think you have some things for me," said the patrol man, looking at Donald.

"Chikitta will get everything. Go on Chikitta – the bag."

In a flash, the little brown monkey was gone and the caravan was peaceful once again.

"One more thing," said Signor Pepperino, his eyes twinkling. "Where were you hiding that monkey? I never did find her."

"In Twitch's hutch; she behaved perfectly."

"Well that makes a change … and now, what about you Bambino. How would you like to perform with Victor Vulcan for the rest of our time in Broadland? He is very impressed with you and is happy to stay with us for the rest of the summer."

Donald nodded happily. He couldn't think of anything he'd like more.

"Well," said the ferryman eventually. "How about supper on the houseboat?"

"Great," said Donald. He could already smell the sizzling sausages and crispy onions beckoning him back to the muddy creek. Soon, Signor Pepperino, the ferryman, Victor Vulcan, the children – as well as Chikitta, Henry, and Twitch were all making their way along the marshy track, over the broken stile, to the houseboat at the side of the river.

Jen and her uncle set to work straight away with the barbecue, while Signor Pepperino poured the elderberry juice. Donald decided to wander along the water's edge.

Suddenly, he heard a familiar *currah currah* sound and a black and white duck, with a grey, speckled crest appeared from amongst the reeds.

"Tufty," he shouted. "Wherever have you been?"

The duck swam back into the reeds, and then reappeared – but he was not alone.

Just behind him was another duck with dark brown feathers; her crest was quite tiny in comparison. Behind this duck came five ducklings.

"Hey look," shouted Donald. "Tufty's gone and found himself a mate."

Jen, Charlie and Josh ran over, just as Tufty glided past; his crest fluttering proudly in the breeze. Chikitta on the other hand didn't seem the slightest bit impressed. She slipped up into the trees and threw furry catkins down into the water. Tufty flapped back at her, while his mate gathered her alarmed brood back together.

"Naughty Chikitta," said Jen. "You mustn't frighten the babies."

Henry opened a sleepy eye from on top of the houseboat and then, with a little white rabbit between his paws, went back to sleep.

The children however were not at all tired, and they enjoyed sausages, chocolate muffins and elderberry juice, which they of course shared with Tufty, Tufty's mate, and their five beautiful ducklings.

Bridge at Potter Heigham

This medieval bridge is an object of great interest, particularly during certain times of the year. Its banks are filled with picnickers and spectators during a week in June when the annual 'Three Rivers Race' takes place. The bridge is a favourite viewing point, where competitors can be seen taking down their masts before venturing underneath.

In the story, it has been renamed Broadshaven Bridge and it becomes the location, where the discovery of the secret scroll takes place.

Marsh End

Marsh End Chalet, on the bank of the River Thurne, is where the mystery begins to unfold. With a little bit of help from a duck and a monkey, the children find out that things are not what they seem.

Also available in the series:

DONALD AND SIGNOR PEPPERINO'S AMAZING CIRCUS

Donald can't believe his luck when he wins a place in Signor Pepperino's Amazing Circus.
The lonely Norfolk marshes become the destination for a most unusual riverside mystery and he soon finds himself involved in an adventure that takes him along waterways, to a mill which holds a secret; a secret that Donald is determined to uncover.